Erik the Viking proves to be a real asset to the U-14s. He's big and he's strong, so much so that manager Joe Duggan is always being asked to produce his birth cert. With new blood like him and Paudie (from Arigna), and old hands like Dave and Bull and Rory, Shannon Harps is right up there with the top U-14 teams.

The girls have had to join an all-girl U-14 team. They're now playing for their old enemies, the townies! But Big Mary's loyalties are still with Shannon Harps and she and Joe concoct a plan to upscuttle Dodgy McHale and his bunch of U-14 big-heads.

Meanwhile, James and Megan take time out from the U-10s to listen to Paddy Joe Padden's endless supply of stories. He feeds them a riddle. What's the difference between May and July? Sadly, they find out in the end …

Peter Regan

sHANNON HARps
A Fresh Start

Illustrated by Terry Myler

THE CHILDREN'S PRESS

To
Peter and Renee Burke

First published 2004 by
The Children's Press
an imprint of Anvil Books
45 Palmerston Road, Dublin 6

1 3 5 6 4 2

ISBN 1 901737 49 7

All characters are fictional.
Any resemblance to real persons, living or dead,
is purely coincidental.

Typeset by Computertype Limited
Printed by Colour Books Limited

Contents

1   Problems   7

2   New Faces   17

3   Arigna   29

4   Big Mary Makes a Splash   38

5   Photo-Calls   48

6   Sligo   57

7   The Big Young Lad   69

8   A Cunning Plot   81

9   The Mystery Tour   93

10   Endings   106

1 Problems

Joe Duggan hummed 'Country Roads', one of his favourite songs, as he drove his Land Rover home from work. It was a fine May evening with hardly a car on the road and sprays of sunshine spilling through the fields and hedgerows. Pretty soon he'd leave the main road and cross over the Shannon into a landscape of newborn meadow grass and roadside dykes. But it wasn't flat. It was hilly and bumpy, with the occasional homestead set on hillocks up narrow laneways off the winding dip of the road. Once or twice he passed the wrecks of former homes: small buttresses of rocks which were once walls, the domains of families long gone who walked the fields' pathways from one farm to the next, from one parish to another.

He had left home early that morning for work but he wouldn't get home for at least another two hours. First he had to go to the new pitch of the team he managed, Shannon

Harps. There was something of a problem about what teams the club would have for the new season. They had hoped to go U-13 and U-10. But the north county section, of which they were part, had stated there would be no U-13 league, that they'd have to skip a year and go U-14. This led to an application from Joe to the County Board to take in two nearby parishes where there weren't enough kids to form their own teams. The Board agreed and the players were released to Shannon Harps.

But U-14 meant another problem. Big Mary Doherty, Josephine Gaffney, Helen Moran and Stella Stephens, the older girls from the parish, would not be allowed to play as there was a rule that girls couldn't play U-14 football on the same team as boys. As there weren't enough girls in the neighbourhood to form a U-14 team that left them with two options: play for some other club that *had* a U-14 girls' team, or get involved with managing the U-10 team.

These were just two of the problems Joe faced as he drove the final mile to Shannon

Harps' new pitch, a mile from the old pitch on the banks of the Shannon.

He was also concerned about the kids from the other two parishes whom he was about to see for the first time. He only hoped there would be some quality, that he wasn't about to be landed with a crowd of no-hopers, barely fit to knock snow off a rope. And that they would integrate with Shannon Harps.

When he drove into the field, he had a quick look about before getting out of the Land Rover. Most of the usual faces were there waiting for him, togged out and having a kickabout. There were a few faces he didn't know – they would be from the other two parishes. They were right at the heart of the kickabout, almost as if they were Shannon Harps through and through. The sight lightened Joe's heart.

The pitch looked perfect. The 'dressing-rooms', the two containers Joe had fitted out during the previous few months, looked the real McCoy.

And the goal-posts! They were tall and

straight, up to county-team standard, newly painted by the two old-timers who helped him, Martin McManus and Jack Gilmartin. There was no sign of either of them. Jack had done Trojan work for the club in the past. So had Martin – Martin, the stuff of football legend and an old county great, a man who had won an All-Ireland Senior Football medal in Croke Park.

'Where are Jack and Martin?' he asked one of the two young kids who had rushed over to the Land Rover.

'We don't know,' replied James Leydon who would be hoping for a place on the U-10 team. His friend Megan Martin was at his side. They went everywhere together. She, too would be in with a good chance of playing U-10 football. Unlike last season when she couldn't figure at all.

'We met Jack in the village an hour ago,' went on James. 'He told me and Megan that he wanted to speak to you in private, that he and Martin have something on their minds and they want to talk it over…There are a good few new players here. None down from

10

Arigna though, we thought there'd be some from there. There are eight for the U-10s and five for the U-14s. I counted every last one of them. I don't know about the U-14s but the U-10s will be super. Mighty is the word Megan used.'

'What's wrong with the U-14s?'

'They're not U-14s. They are all U-13!'

'Where are the girls? Big Mary? Stella? Josephine? Helen?'

'They're in the dressing-rooms.'

'What are they doing there?'

'Sulking, I think.'

'Here give me a hand to get the gear out of the Land Rover.'

As soon as Joe opened the back of the Land Rover to get out the training equipment and more footballs, Dave Gilboy, Rory Gilmartin (Jack's nephew) and Bull Malone were over like a flash.

'Four of the new lot are pretty good, Joe,' said Rory. 'But there's not one U-14 among them, they're all U-13s.'

'So James tells me. Set up the cones for me, will you?'

'We'll get trounced playing U-14 football,' added Dave.

'Look on the bright side. You'll have a team to play for, that's what matters…now James here says Big Mary and Stella are sulking. I want to find out what's wrong. Give me a few minutes till I sort them out.'

When Joe got to the dressing-rooms Big Mary and Stella looked at him as if he were a no-hoper. And that was exactly how he felt as he stood in front of them, all hot and bothered after a hard day's work roofing a house down Mohill way, overlooking a lake that would be a pure dream once the lunch-time break came.

'What's bothering you two?' he asked.

'Nothing that would interest you in the slightest,' snapped Stella Stephens.

Joe was slightly shaken. It wasn't like Stella, one of the best Gaelic footballers for her age in the country, to act nasty.

'You don't care about us,' she went on. 'There should be room for us to play on with Shannon Harps. It's not fair that we have to get out just because there's a rule that's says

12

we can't stay on with the rest of the team after U-12 level. It's plain stupid.'

'Listen, Stella, I didn't make the rules. But I have to go by them. It's rough but that's the way it is… Where are the rest?'

'Helen says she couldn't be bothered. Josephine says there's no point if we can't be on the team any more. She's right. What's the point? It just isn't fair. We've done a lot to get Shannon Harps started. The four of us worked hard organising events and getting money in. And now we're out. And all because of a stupid anti-girl rule. It's ridiculous. If we had our own girls' team it wouldn't be so bad. But we haven't. We've nothing any more and now we're being forced into a corner.'

'What do you mean? Nobody is forcing you into a corner.'

'Joe Duggan, that's where you're mistaken!' Big Mary Doherty had joined the discussion. There was thunder in her voice, a kind of raging lightning in her eyes. 'All we've ever wanted was to play for Shannon Harps. Fine if we had the numbers to form a girls' team. But we haven't.

'Because of that we should be allowed to stay on the team. But we can't because of this stupid rule. The townies have got wind of what's going on. They've started up a girls' team and want us to play for them. They say there'd be no problems. D'ye hear that, Mister Joe Duggan! The townies! No doubt they'll want us to spy on you. Find out what's going on.'

'I wouldn't put it past them!' nodded Joe.

The townies were their arch-rivals. Just to mention the name was sure to set the blood boiling. Only the season before Shannon Harps had had a run-in with them. The U-12 cup final between the two teams had led to a protest and a load of trouble.

'We're thinking of joining the townies,' gestured Big Mary.

'That's why we came here. To tell you,' added Stella.

'How about Helen and Josephine?'

'They're thinking of joining too.'

'Have you told the others about this?'

'No. We wanted to tell you first. Anyway, it's not our fault. What else is there.'

'You could give a hand to run the U-10s.'

'Joe Duggan, we want none of that. We want to play football, not look on.'

'Are you coming out to train then?'

'No. We're finished with Shannon Harps. We'll be doing all our training with the townies from now on. That's the way it is.'

Before Joe could reply the two girls turned and walked away.

Joe watched them go. He'd miss them. Shannon Harps would too. They'd done great work for the club. Helped get it on its feet. All four had worked wonders. What a way for everything to end!

Joe wasn't in much humour to take training. He should have been, especially with all the new kids to sift through. But the talk with the girls had knocked him for six. He called Dave over.

'Dave, you, Bull and Rory take training.'

'Why? What's up with you?'

'I want to see Martin McManus.'

'Can't it wait?'

'No. It's urgent. I'm off.'

He climbed into the Land Rover and drove off. He was glad to get away from the field. Hopefully, a few minutes of open road driving would clear his mind of his disappointment over the girls. He'd either catch Martin and Jack on the road or over at Martin's house. Joe felt there was something wrong there as well. What a day! He still hadn't got home from work or had time for a bite to eat.

Life as a football manager – what a headache!

2 New Faces

Joe got to Martin McManus's house within minutes. Jack Gilmartin was there, sitting at the kitchen table having a cup of tea.

'I've a few problems, Martin. The girls have left. They're joining the townies.'

'Can't blame them. There's nothing for them with us. Jack and I have been thinking of throwing it in too.'

'Martin, don't even dream of it! I need you. Your experience. You're the only ones around here who know anything worthwhile about the game. We'd be lost without the two of you.'

What Joe Duggan said was mainly true. Martin and Jack were two old-timers who knew the game inside out. And not just from the playing end of matters, but from the administrative, rules and regulations side. They knew how the game was run from top to bottom. They were two wily old foxes, especially Martin, who had spent a lifetime around the game.

'Did many new kids show up from the other two parishes for training?' asked Jack Gilmartin.

'A few. About as many as I thought.'

'Did they send down any adults to help?'

'Not one.'

'See! No help. They've just dumped the kids. Why should we look after them? We'd be as well giving up if we can't supply enough players from our own parish.'

'I don't want to be going into that again.'

'Well, if they don't bother, why should we?'

'It's not the kids' fault. All they want to do is play football.'

'Are they any use?'

'I wouldn't know. I just got there. One thing for sure, the older ones are a bit young for U-14. It's one disaster after another.'

'It's not all bad news,' said Martin. He took an envelope off the mantelpiece.

'What is it?'

'A letter inviting Shannon Harps to take part in an U-13 Feile Na Gael tournament in

Sligo. It's to be run over a weekend. You'll be put up in a hostel. I don't know how the letter is addressed to me as you're the club secretary. But that's the way it is. Are you interested?'

The letter brought a smile to Joe's face.

'This is great. We'll go for sure. I wonder who else will be playing?'

'Whoever, they'll all be quality. They only ask the best. It's a real honour.'

'A sure tonic. Do you want to come up to the field and see what's what?'

'No, you go on your own. It's not our place to be there.'

'Does that mean you're giving up?'

'It could.'

Joe had an afterthought. 'Jack, we've three great prospects: Bull Malone, Dave Gilboy and your nephew. Are you going to leave him out in the cold? Not pass on your knowledge of the game? He's come on a ton this last year. The first time I saw him he was raw. But with Martin's coaching he's turned the corner. A lot of people are sitting up and taking notice of him, not just from here but all around the county – and in Leitrim on account of his school team. He's on the verge of having that little extra something that'll make him special, the same with the two other lads. You owe it to the kids to help them. There are things they can learn from the two of you that they won't learn anywhere else. Don't let them down.'

'Joe Duggan, you've a nice way of putting things,' said Martin slowly. 'But…'

'I think we should help,' said Jack softly.

'Maybe we should.'

'What does that mean?'

'We'll help.'

'Are you coming back to the field then?'

'Not now. But we'll be down soon as you have all the new players sorted out.'

'Is that a promise?'

'Of course.'

Back at the pitch, Dave, Rory and Bull had everyone doing laps of the field – the U-10s lapping one way, the others the opposite. Bull was in charge of the U-10s.

'There's no point in them all running all

together. They're two different teams and that's the way it should be from the start.'

'But they're the one club, Shannon Harps,' reminded Rory.

'Sure, but on account of the age gap, they'll bond better as teams if treated separately, especially with all those new kids on board.'

'There are some good ones on the U-10 panel,' continued Bull. 'James and Megan are toppers. Maybe Joe will let me be their trainer. I could work wonders with them. I've found out enough about football this last year to train any class of team. Sure, there's nothing to it; just a firm hand and plenty of shouting. I'd be up to that class of carry-on, no bother.'

'Maybe you would. But would they be up to you?' said Rory, grinning.

'What's that supposed to mean?'

'Bull, you're too much of a messer to be a trainer. They wouldn't take you seriously. You'd only have them going half-an-hour before you'd start. Then they would all mess. It'd be a comedy show.'

'So you think.'

'So I know.'

When Joe Duggan got back from seeing Jack and Martin, Bull broached the matter.

'I wouldn't be fully thinking that way,' replied Joe Duggan.

'Does that leave me out?' asked Bull.

'No, you could give a hand. You and Jack could look after the U-10s. That would leave me and Martin to take the U-14s.'

'That'll be pure cool,' purred Bull. 'I have all kinds of tricks up me sleeve. The opposition won't have a clue what's going on.'

'That's what I'm afraid of. And that's why I want Jack there. To keep an eye on you!'

Joe couldn't have said a truer word. Bull couldn't let an hour pass without getting into some kind of mischief.

Bull pretended not to hear. 'Let's have a bit of a trial match. I'll ref. That way you can have a look at what's on offer.'

'Good idea,' glowed Joe. 'Give it fifteen minutes a side. Let Dave and Rory pick the two teams. Mix both U-10s and U-14s together. You ref. Dave and Rory can act as captains. I'll sit back and scribble a few notes, write down what I make of the new lot. Don't pick James on a team. I need him on the sideline to put names to faces. He knows most of the kids from the other two parishes. He can tell me who's who.'

Dave and Rory picked the two teams and got them out on the pitch. As Bull lined them up for the throw-in, he quickly realised that with the profuse mix of football jerseys it wouldn't be easy to tell the two teams apart.

He called a halt and, between training bibs and an exchange of jerseys, got Dave's team near enough to wearing the one colour. As for Rory's team they were a total mix of liquorice allsorts.

The opening few minutes were scrappy enough. There was very little linkage, with most movements breaking down almost as soon as they started. This didn't disappoint Joe a lot. It was early days and once the new players got used to one another they'd build up a better understanding and their team-work would become more fluid.

It became obvious after a few minutes that three of the new players, although U-13, were real prospects. As James was filling in their names, Joe's mind was busy planning where he'd use them.

Tommy Doran would be ideal teamed up in midfield with Rory Gilmartin. He was big and strong, and a great kicker of a ball from his hands. His fielding was also top-class and it was almost impossible to knock him about, thus doing away with the possibility of the ball being spilled.

The second player to catch his eye was Tony Shine, whom he saw in the full-back position; this would release Bull to play full-forward on a regular basis.

The third player was Joey McDermott, a neat footballer who seemed to have that little extra bit of know-how; he'd fill in anywhere across the half-back line. He was a good reader of the game and was very quick about the pitch.

A fourth player also caught his eye.

'Who's your man?' he asked James.

'The fellow with a sweat band?'

'Is that what it is? Who is he?'

'He's Eric Higgins. He's more football in his blood than most.'

'What do you mean?'

'He likes to play rugby as well.'

'Is that what's with the sweat band?'

'Yes. He wears it all the time, once he's playing football.'

'There's no rugby played anywhere near here. Not unless he goes into the fields and plays with the cows.'

'That's what he does. He has his own ball

and plays with that.'

'Plays with the cows?'

'No, with Tommy and Tony. He's very rough though.'

'I can see that. He's a referee's nightmare. Still, there's room for him on any team I have. Are you sure he's underage? He looks like a half-man who should be playing Minor football for Cork.'

'He's well underage. He's only thirteen.'

'All the same, there'll be nothing but protests flying all over the place. What did you say his name is?'

'Higgins. Eric Higgins. They call him "Eric the Viking". He lives beside the Shannon. His house is fit for a millionaire. The gardens are huge and there's a big jetty. His da is an architect and has his own cruiser. Bull says the reason he's called Eric the Viking is because he's got Viking blood. His ancestors came to Ireland on long boats from Norway, sailed up the river Shannon and never left. They're still here.

'Eric's real quiet off the pitch, quiet as a lamb. But once he's togged out he's fierce and as loud as thunder. And he really wants to be part of Shannon Harps. He'll be great to have. Everyone will be afraid of him. They'll be that afraid they'll give him the ball rather than be tackled by him. He's super doing rugby tackles.'

'He's a find. Once he understands there are no rugby tackles in Gaelic, I'll just turn him loose.'

Out on the pitch the standard of play had improved, the passing and cohesion were a lot more fluid. Joe was heartened by the U-10s on view – they were all up to scratch. Whatever about winning a trophy, it would take a good team to beat them.

He would have felt the same about the older age group – if they had been in a U-13 league.

Just then he remembered the letter Martin had given him about the U-13 tournament in Sligo. He was in two minds whether to tell the players about it but he decided not to. He'd hold it back until after the next training session. Wait until he was clearer in his own mind as to how the team would shape up.

Then he thought of what James had said earlier about no Arigna players showing up.

'Does us a favour, James?'

'What?'

'There must be some players in Arigna. I haven't much time. Will you drop up there in the next few days, have a look around, and if there's anything of use ask them to come down so as we can look at them?'

'Surely. I'll get Megan to go with me.'

On the way from training Joe gave some of the new players a lift in the Land Rover.

He thought of asking Eric the Viking too, only he had a bike with him.

As he watched him cycle away, Joe had the silly thought that, more fittingly, Eric should be coming and going by boat.

Silly but possible.

Being a football manager, Joe Duggan knew all about both.

3 Arigna

The following afternoon, soon as the bell went for the end of the school day, James and Megan got their bikes out and cycled to Arigna on the lookout for likely prospects to play for Shannon Harps.

Megan wanted to bring Jimeen, their donkey, but James would have none of it.

'He'd only slow us up. We'll use our bikes. It'll be much quicker and Jimeen can take it easy. It's all he's fit for nowadays.'

'I suppose you're right. Maybe I'll take him down to the lake when we get back. He'll like that. I can put him on the long rope and let him wander about.'

'Don't let him into the water. It's too muddy.'

'I'm not that silly. I'll keep him well back. Maybe bring a bucket and splash water over him. He loves that.'

James smiled. Although Jimeen was his, Megan was totally crazy about him. She went to see him every day and not a dry one went by that she didn't bring him out for a trot, especially along the woodland paths that flanked the lake.

The lake, its crannog, and the graveyard a little way down the road, the holy well and the derelict castle a mile away, were the places James and Megan most liked to play. It was known as Kilronan.

Paddy Joe Padden, who in their eyes was the oldest man in the whole of Ireland, told them how it got its name. It came from the Irish: 'the church of Ronan'. Ronan was a monk who had lived centuries before, He had built a church on an island in the lake and turned the general area into a place of meditation and prayer. Paddy Joe was great for telling stories of times long ago. James and Megan always visited him and intended doing so on their way home from Arigna.

Arigna was once a mining village, with anthracite mines that gave employment to hundreds of part-time workers. They cycled long miles from their farms in winter rain and summer sun to spend gruelling hours underground. For some, a round trip constituted up to twenty miles, no joke when soaked through from the rain. At the pit there was no change of clothes, or chance of a shower.

But the mines were long closed. All that was left now was a small cluster of houses and a church set on the side of a mountain. Beside the church was a graveyard that must have been the steepest in the whole of Ireland. Where the ground levelled off at the bottom of the village there was a small football pitch, only yards away from a colossal storage yard and a closed-up mine head with overhead cables, huge open-ended corrugated sheds and slag heaps that even winter rain couldn't move.

When James and Megan got to the village there was no one at the football pitch. The village looked empty too. There wasn't much to be seen except the dull black of slag and coal dust everywhere.

James got Megan to knock on a few doors and in about ten minutes they had six young fellows down to the football pitch. Luckily they brought a ball as James and Megan had forgotten to. All but two of them were U-10. The two older ones, Ned and Paudie, were spot on for the U-14s, meaning they were underage by only a few months. More to the point, they were strong and sturdy; they would be certain to make the team They said they went to school in Drumshanbo with Bull, Dave and Rory.

That piece of news made James and Megan feel a little cross. Here they were going out of their way to unearth players for Shannon Harps and it seemed that Bull, Dave and Rory hadn't even gone to the bother of letting it be known in school that the club was looking for players.

'We'll have a kickabout and see how things go,' said James.

'It won't be much of a kickabout with only seven playing,' retorted Paudie.

'Megan here plays too.'

'A girl!'

'She's as good as any fellow.'

'That could be so. Isn't that Big Mary one from down your way?'

'She is surely. And you wouldn't want to be calling her Big Mary. Not to her face.'

'Right you are. What's your name?'

'James. And this here is Megan.'

'Well, James,' said Ned, 'we'll mix two teams and use half the pitch.'

'Another thing,' he added, 'with so few playing we'll do away with goal-posts altogether and only use coats. There'll be no goal-keepers as such. Anyone can stand in as they see fit. One rule applies: ball along the ground to score. That way, there'll be no rowing over points, or height for a goal.'

James was wondering how the two teams would know what side they were on. He soon got an answer.

'We'll have a toss for it. The team that loses plays without tops.'

'You mean take their shirts and vests off?'

'Sure. No big deal. The sun is shining, isn't it?'

Paudie and Ned, the seniors, were made captains. James was on Paudie's team and Megan on Ned's.

Very soon, James could see that three of

the U-10s were useful. But he guessed Shannon Harps would have to take the fourth on board if they wanted the others.

However, Paudie and Ned were the real stars. Even allowing for the advantage of the age difference. Almost every time they got the ball, apart from when they confronted one another, there was no contest. They fielded and soloed to their hearts' content, scoring at will. They would both be a definite asset to Shannon Harps.

'Why don't you all come down to our new pitch for training next Tuesday?' asked James

34

when the kickabout was over.

'We'll do that, no bother,' said Paudie. 'Are you sure it's U-14?'

'We wouldn't be here if it wasn't. Well, that and looking out for U-10s as well.'

'Are you happy enough with these lads?'

He pointed to the clutch of four. 'They're all there is at U-10 around here. Two of them are only nine. Big nines though.'

'Is there anyone else you know around here who might like to play?'

'Well, there's Gerry Flynn. Lives over at Mount Allen. You can't miss the house. It's right beside the road, with an orchard next to it. Be careful going up to the house. There's a dog. Gerry Flynn is a fine player. U-13. He plays best in the half-forward line. I'll ask him, if you like, bring him along on Tuesday. What do you think?'

'Fine. See you Tuesday then?'

'We'll be there no matter what.'

James and Megan got on their bikes and freewheeled downhill, the smooth sheen of Lough Allen receding from view almost as rapidly as their descent.

In next to no time they were in the vicinity of Mount Allen where Gerry Flynn lived. James decided to drop in on him – just in case the others didn't.

'Like to play for Shannon Harps?' James asked, when he appeared.

'Sure enough. But why isn't Bull Malone doing the asking? We're in the same class at school. It should be up to him, or the manager, not a youngster like you. Though I wouldn't mind playing, if it was allowed. I heard what happened last year to that lad you played from Galway. I was at the final where they wouldn't give you the medals. I don't want that to happen to me.'

'There isn't a problem. It's been cleared for anyone in this parish to play for us – once they're the right age.'

'Did you ask anyone else?'

'We were up the hill and got a few there,' put in Megan.

'Up in Arigna?'

'Yes, we got some U-10s and two, Ned and Paudie, for U-14. They're super.'

'They're that and all. Did they say they'd

go to training on Tuesday?'

'Yes. They're cycling down.'

'Tell you what – I'll go with them. What time is training at?'

'Half-seven. The new pitch.'

'I know it…I'll be there.'

'You don't know any one else who might be interested?'

'No. You've got them all as it is.'

James and Megan got back on their bikes and headed off down on their way to Paddy Joe Padden.

Gerry Flynn turned and went around the back of the house to feed the 'Seven Sisters' – meaning the seven hens in the henhouse, one of his many chores.

See, Gerry Flynn, like most of Shannon Harps players was a country boy true and true.

What else could he be, living west of the Shannon.

4 Big Mary Makes a Splash

Football matters seen to, James and Megan called on Paddy Joe.

Paddy was a great man for telling stories that were handed down by word of mouth and never recorded in any book.

He had great old sayings too, like, 'It could be a hungry July', meaning while new crops were still growing in the fields old crops could run out if matters weren't properly planned in advance.

And another: 'A wet May and a dry June makes the farmer whistle a happy tune.'

And a sarcastic one: 'Those who cannot work without a hump: Tailors, writers and cats.'

But the one that Megan particularly liked was: 'The donkey is the poor man's horse.'

'What's got the pair of you out and about?' asked Paddy Joe.

'Nothing much. We just dropped in for a chat.'

'Once it's not to do with chasing a bag of wind around a field. I can't see an ounce of sense in that kind of carry-on. It's a waste of good working time.'

'Oh, we just want to hear some stories. Your kind of stories.'

'What I'll tell you now is the truth. These days people have lost the run of themselves, what with fancy houses, fancy cars and fancy notions. But that wasn't the way I had it, or my mother and father either, or theirs. They had to work from first light to dark to make do, to put food on the table and keep hold of the land. Their parents before them had it even worse, toiling in the same fields going back to times when they didn't have title. Instead their land belonged, as did all the land around here, to a landlord. They had to pay rent and if they didn't they were thrown out and a new tenant put in their place. It was only in later years people got to own their land.'

'Who was the landlord around here?' asked Megan.

'Tenison.'

'Did he own the old castle over at Kilronan?'

'The very one. The Tenisons lived there for years. They weren't the worst as landlords went. The castle and grounds were full of splendour. There was hardly a more beautiful place in the whole county. It was fit for royalty. Not that many of our kind saw the inside of it, except to do the work.'

'It wouldn't be much good to royalty now. The place is falling down. There isn't even a roof on it.'

'Shame! The Tenisons left about the late 1930s. They sold the place on. It was left empty. The lead was stripped from the roof and sold. That and pure neglect. Sometimes change isn't always for the best. But I like to think it's better these days, even if the castle is in ruins – sure haven't we got hundreds of castles all over the place. People now own their own homes, not like years ago when they just about owned the clothes they stood in. No, sad as the castle looks, it's all for the better, once people don't lose the run of themselves.'

'Has the castle any ghost stories?'

'A few. But I won't tell you now. Some other time.'

'When?'

'When I'm not so tired. I need to rest.'

'Sorry…'

And they were sorry. Because Paddy Joe Padden was one very old man. He was slowing down a lot lately. It wasn't fair of them to be pestering him.

Paddy Joe watched them leave and went back into the house. True he was tired, but not as tired as he made out to be. Megan had triggered old memories to do with the struggle for the land. Memories he rarely discussed, and certainly not with children.

These days he found it hard to remember. Sometimes he couldn't recall faces or names or places. Was there ever such a past?

Yes, there was, and it was up to him to make sure the struggle of a people would never be taken for granted.

Big Mary, Stella, Josephine and Helen almost didn't get to play for the townies. At first, they didn't like the set-up.

The trouble started when some of the boys from the U-12s of the previous season began to slag Big Mary. They were still into their 'Ita Little' (eat a little) jeering routine. Big Mary flew off the handle and grabbed one of them by the jumper and horsed him into the local river. There was a bit of a drop and a strong flow. The lad made quite a splash and only there was a lifebuoy nearby he would have got into serious difficulties. He was quickly hauled out only for Big Mary to threaten to throw him back in again.

Stella, the only one capable of calming Big Mary once her temper got out of control, had to step in and with a little help from Helen and Josephine got her away from her tormentors.

Word of the incident got back to the club. One of the committee was incensed – the boy who ended up in the river was his son. An apology was demanded from Big Mary. It wasn't forthcoming. Acting true to form, the others stood by her. They didn't go near the club for a few weeks. Then some of the girls

on the team came looking for them.

'Don't mind those chaps. They think they're macho. They're mostly dumb-bells with fresh air between their ears.'

'They're proper big-heads. They slag us too.'

'We hate the sight of them. Just as much as your Shannon Harps does. Most of the kids in our club are okay. It's just that lot. They're poison. Forget what happened, just come back. We'll look after you. It won't happen again. You have our word.'

But Big Mary wasn't convinced. 'Some

people have long memories – that long they'd make great historians. What's to say that the slagging won't start again if we go back?'

'You have our word. Anyway the committee won't let it happen.'

'Like that Sean Beirne?'

'Don't worry about him. That's all in the past.'

Sean Beirne belonged to the past, but not the distant past. He had been one of the central figures in the row over the U-12 cup final the previous season. His name wasn't flavour of the month with Shannon Harps and never would be. Football teams never forget – they only remember.

There was bound to be a carry-over to the new season, especially as the teams would be competing almost en-block at the U-14 age level.

'Are you coming back, or not? There's no point in bearing a grudge, and everyone wants to have you back.'

'We'd like to think it over first.'

'That's your choice. Take a week.'

Big Mary and the others took the full week

to make up their minds and their decision was to go back to the townies. It took a while for the uneasiness to disappear, but it did. The girls settled in and gave their all, just as they had for done for Shannon Harps.

There was no more slagging. It was a thing of the past.

One day a letter arrived in the post for the townies' secretary.

The letter was from the County Juvenile Selection Committee detailing both Big Mary and Stella to attend a training session in Elphin where they would be considered for the girls' U-14 county team.

Both were delighted with the news.

Word travelled quickly around the village about their good fortune. A few days later Stella was standing outside the village shop when Martin pulled up in his car.

'I just heard the news, Stella. It's great, even though you're playing for a different club now. I wish you the best of luck.'

'Thanks, Martin. A lot of it is down to the coaching you gave us last year. It wouldn't have happened only for you and Jack.'

'I don't know about that. Don't forget Joe Duggan, he got the team going. If it weren't for him there would be no Shannon Harps. No starting point for you.'

Stella paused. She gave Martin a hard stare, almost as if she didn't fully agree with what he had just said.

'Stella, you don't seem to care much about Joe. How's that?'

'It's not that. It's…'

Her voice faltered. She couldn't finish the sentence. How could she tell Martin she thought Joe Duggan was a bit of an eejit?

Another village old-timer was standing outside the shop and had heard what was going on. He got his sixpence worth in.

'Don't judge the book by the cover. Just because Joe hasn't any fancy talk doesn't mean you should despise him. Sure he's done more work for Shannon Harps than God himself. And a lot of it paid out of his own pocket. And, Martin, you know where Joe Duggan came from: a family of seven children brought up on the side of a rocky hill with barely a roof over their heads and four walls to keep the wind out. He's come on well in life. Look at him now, a big car and fine house, and all his own. As good a carpenter or handyman as is in the county. He's going from strength from strength. And more power to him. No, young girl, you should have respect for Joe Duggan.'

Stella got something of a shock on hearing about Joe's background of poverty. She quickly waved to Martin and was gone.

One thing sure; she'd have plenty of sympathy for Joe from now on.

And who was the old-timer who had sprung to Joe's defence?

None other than Bull Malone's grand-father.

5 Photo-Calls

Officially the season hadn't begun yet, but Joe organised a few friendly games in advance of the tournament in Sligo. He wasn't interested in results, more in seeing how the players blended together and interplayed as a team. A few rough edges needed sorting out on both teams, so he and Martin were only too happy to have a few weeks' grace before having to face other teams in competition.

Joe had also to organise a photo-call in *The Cross Bar*, the local pub belonging to Dave's father, to publicise Shannon Harps' new strip. It would be blue as before, but with additional red flashing on the sleeves as well as a black trimming on the football togs to represent the parishes the new players were from. Joe had to lay on a photographer and reporter from the local newspaper, as well as some players.

As things turned out the photo-call in *The Cross Bar* wasn't the only one Joe attended

48

during that week. He had been called to a new job about ten miles from home and was well pleased with what he saw — a derelict mansion with plenty of outhouses, all half in ruins. The idea was to knock the lot and build a mix of apartments and detached houses instead. Joe could see two good years of work and much needed money staring him in the face.

Word about the project had gone out to all kinds of protestors, some of them from as far away as Dublin, and by some not-so-strange-coincidence all these groups had arrived on site at much the same time as Joe.

He was puzzled by what he saw.

The protestors were divided into two camps: those for and those against the new scheme. The developer, the builder and some workers stood on one side of the driveway that led to the mansion, together with some local representatives of the Irish Farmers' Association. The protesters, who were a crowd of almost total strangers, stood on the opposite verge of the driveway.

The gardai were also present. But they had

decided on a low-key approach, while keeping on the alert for trouble. Already they had the likely ringleaders sourced. A few arm-locks wouldn't go amiss. That and a heavy reprimand should suffice to break up any trouble. Meanwhile they were enjoying the fine sweep of rural landscape.

'What's all the fuss?' asked Joe of one member of the Irish Farmers' Association.

'Fuss isn't the word! It's a crying shame! All these crowds, almost total strangers, coming here and trying to put a block on a local development. We're sick of it! We've had enough! It's got so bad we're not even allowed to build houses for own families on the land we own, over being dictated to by a crowd from Dublin. They're an army of do-good idlers who have nothing on their minds except block every planning application in the country. I wouldn't mind but they're from every corner of the country except here. The cheek! The impudence!'

'What's their case?'

'Case? I have a better class of name for it. They're going on about a rare breed of bat.

The ruins of the mansion and outhouses have been full of bats for years. But now, all of a sudden, when something positive is being done for the area, the bats have become a rare species and need to be protected. It wouldn't make a blight of a difference to knock the place. The bats will move on and bring their rarity with them. Sure, isn't the country full of old ruins and empty houses, not to mention a crowd of empty-headed lousers from Dublin.'

And that was the read according to one angry protester.

Suddenly, a JCB came into view from around a bend in the driveway. It was being driven at full-throttle, making a beeline for the front of the mansion.

A ferocious cheer of approval rose from the pro-building side.

There was a groan of disbelief from the antis.

Then the gardai swung into action.

First in the firing line was the JCB driver.

A protestor somehow got a hold on the frame of the cab and hauled himself up, taking the driver by surprise. He switched off the ignition and pocketed the key, bringing the JCB to a halt just yards from the mansion.

There followed a free for all. Building workers, farmers, pro- and anti-protestors, gardai, were all caught up in it.

It was simply one huge tidal wave of angry people and Joe was dragged into the middle of it. The only one who didn't get caught up was a lone press photographer who took a lovely action photo of Joe, arm out, appearing to knock the cap off a garda.

Before matters got much further out of hand everybody came to their senses and trudged off in their various groupings. Luckily, no summonses ensued. The project was left on the long finger. And the bats still survive in the derelict ivy-filled world of the mansion and outhouses.

The press coverage wasn't quite what Joe had planned.

The following Thursday *The Cross Bar* photo of him holding one of the new jerseys appeared in the *Roscommon Herald*. It was on one of the inside sports pages. Only sports

fans would have seen it.

But the large photo on Page One was a scorcher. Nobody in the whole county could have missed it. It showed Joe grappling with a garda, the one who lost his cap.

There was also a full-page report detailing the protest and the plight of the bats.

It went down a treat with most people, especially the townies. Some of them were inspired to give Joe a new nickname:

BATMAN!

And on account of their unfortunate teammate who ended up in the river, they dragged Big Mary into the equation: the title

BATMAN AND ROBIN.

A week later James and Megan paid Paddy Joe Padden a visit. They coaxed him into telling a story about the castle in Kilronan.

'There was a man named Henry Loane who worked there as a butler. One night he went to bed, only to be woken by the sound of noise in the kitchen. When he went in there were five of them – meaning ghosts – sitting round the table having a chat.'

'What were they talking about?'

'Ah, ye know. Heaven and Hell, that kind of crack. Henry stood listening to them, but they didn't pass a divil of heed on him. When they were done they walked out the door and left. The next night they were back again, and the night after, and all the time it was Heaven and Hell. And how with all the time they spent talking about Heaven and Hell they were in neither one nor the other.

'Thick and all as Henry was the penny

finally dropped. He told them he'd get a priest to come and rest their souls. But they said they weren't in need of a priest. They went on that they were five brothers who had been evicted in the 1850s and had come to return the key of their holding to the lord of the castle.

'They had kept the key in defiance. They had travelled the world homeless and had nothing but bad luck. They felt that until they returned the key their spirits wouldn't be at peace. With that they took this big rusty key and left it on the kitchen table and walked out the door. The five ghosts were never seen nor heard of again. The one certainty was that it was to Heaven or Hell they were gone and they wouldn't be bothering Henry Loane any more.'

'What happened to the key?'

'I have it here in the house.'

'Can we see it?'

Paddy Joe left the room and came back with what was truly a large rusty old key.

'I'll treasure this until the day I die,' he said.

'Why?'

'The five ghosts were the children of my ancestors. They had always wanted to come back but were never able to. Their tale is long and troublesome. They were never at peace. Not until the day that they returned the key.'

It was some story – Paddy Joe Padden style.

6 Sligo

The long awaited weekend of the Feile Na Gael U-13 football blitz in Sligo town finally arrived but unfortunately Martin wasn't able to make it. Dave and Big Mary's dads made an express run the thirty odd miles to Sligo with the bulk of the players, while Joe hitched a trailer to the Land Rover and loaded up with the rest of the players and the gear. They all set out in a convoy at eight o'clock on the Saturday morning.

Basically the panel was confined to the players who had kicked off in the league the previous week. All except Paudie and Ned from Arigna. As U-14s they were overage for the tournament and ineligible to play on a U-13 team.

The convoy arrived in Sligo town by nine o'clock. They crossed over to the far side of town, close to the college grounds where the tournament was to be held, pulled in for a while so as to stretch their legs and had something to eat. Then, having made a few enquiries, they headed off to the college.

They arrived at ten o'clock, to find some of the other teams and officials already there. There were to be eight teams, divided into two sections of four, and they would be competing on a league basis, with the top two teams in each section going through to the semi-finals. The last game in each section, along with the semi-finals and final, were to be played on the Sunday. All the other matches were to be completed by Saturday evening. The format was 13-a-side, with the probability of a two-man full-back line and the same in the full-forward line. All games would be fifteen minutes each way.

Surprise, big surprise, the townies hadn't been invited to compete. Joe had been full certain they would have been top of the list to be invited but he was told that Shannon Harps was the only Roscommon team in the competition. Four, including the host club, were from various parts of county Sligo. The remaining three were from Ballina in Mayo, Bundoran in south Donegal and Manorhamilton in Leitrim.

Shannon Harps were drawn in Section 'B' along with the host club, a team from Tubbercurry and the Manorhamilton outfit.

Section 'A' comprised Enniscrone, Bally-mote, Ballina and Bundoran.

By half-ten all the teams had arrived at the venue. They clustered about the two giant-sized boards that listed the two sections and the order of play. Some of the players arrived already togged out. Others left their kit lying about the place and gave the college grounds and the two football pitches a thorough look-over. A few of the teams knew one another from before and gave quick nods of recognition. Others kept to themselves, keeping their energy for the start of the games.

The host club had everything arranged to a tee. The dressing-rooms were already open and available. There was an amplification system in place and yards of bunting. Refreshments, under the sign 'Little Sid's Mobile Diner', had also arrived, with lots in the way of sweets, minerals and crisps, with burgers and chips for later in the day. Plenty of stewards were on hand to deal with the expected big crowds.

There was to be an extra bonus that day: a Puc Fada competition for all players who wouldn't make it to the semi-final stage.

The dressing-rooms were big but as there were only four it was agreed that there would have to be a double-up with two teams sharing, each drawn from a different section. Shannon Harps got to share with the team from Bundoran.

For the first game, against Tubbercurry, Joe didn't have a problem picking the team. It was pretty much on the lines of the one he had chosen for their opening league fixture a few days previously. In that game Shannon Harps had scraped a win, not bad for a team who, except for two players, were giving away a year in age difference.

Now his major problem wasn't the team. It had to do with his own self-confidence. Here he was, thirty miles away from home, without the guiding hand of either Martin or Jack. He'd have to cope on his own, make the right decisions and inspire the players.

It wouldn't be easy, though he was far from being the rookie manager he had been a year ago when he first founded Shannon Harps. Proof of his lack of status was that when the other teams had arrived none of the managers had even said hello to him. Implied: they had never heard of him. Still, he reminded himself, this was a high prestige affair. Someone, somewhere, must have thought Shannon Harps was a good team. If not, they wouldn't have been invited to mix with some of the best from Sligo, Mayo, Leitrim and Donegal.

Shannon Harps lined out on Pitch 2, the ball was thrown in and the match against Tubbercurry began. They started strongly and were three points to the good before Shannon Harps put a point on the board: a high, curling point from Dave in the right-half-forward position.

Tubbercurry quickly responded with a short passing build-up that led to a point-blank shot rocketing over the bar for what should have been a goal instead of a point.

Then Gerry Flynn, one of the new Shannon Harps players James and Megan had acquired, tracked back from the left-half-forward position and intercepted a sloppy Tubbercurry pass. He soloed forward on a twenty-metre run, played the ball close to the fourteen-metre line where Bull crisply fielded it, feinted and took a few strides forward before unleashing an unstoppable shot into the top corner of the Tubbercurry net.

From then on, anything that was played into Bull in the two-man full-forward line caused havoc. He played a real live-wire role along with his quick-silver partner, Joey McDermott, who'd be a model for top-of-the-left in the 15-a-side game.

At half-time Shannon Harps held a two points lead: 1-6 to 0-7.

Man-of-the-Match, so far, had been Rory, playing his usual commanding midfield role. Tommy Doran, another of the new players, played alongside him and though he played quite well, Joe saw Ned, the U-14 from Arigna, as Rory's natural midfield partner for the duration of the season.

Another new player, Tommy Shine at full-back, was having a very steady game. Nothing flash, unlike his name. But he was making all the right moves, oozing reliability, making no errors.

Eric the Viking didn't come on until the second half at right-half-back. When he appeared, tongues began to wag.

'He's a hairy looking U-13,' muttered the Tubbercurry bench.

'He'd pass for an escort in the Rose of Tralee.'

'Or what was waiting for Jack the giant-

killer at the top of the Beanstalk.'

'And what was that?'

'A giant, thick-head.'

'We could sure do with seeing his birth cert. There are minors not as big. Just look at him. Might as well run into a brick wall.'

And in truth there was no way past Eric the Viking; it was better to get rid of the ball. Some of the Tubbercurry players found this out the hard way and ended up flattened on the ground.

Even the referee got nosey about Eric. He halted the game and spoke to him.

Joe was over in a flash. 'Ref, that's none of your affair. You're here to ref the match and nothing else.'

The Tubbercurry manager wasn't giving way. 'He's sure one big juvenile, let alone U-13. I'd like to see his birth cert.'

'Well, you certainly can't see it now. I'll get someone to bring it tomorrow. And when I do, he'll still be U-13.'

'Bring it then. And what's more, pin it up where it can be seen because the other teams will be just as suspicious. He's the biggest looking U-13 this side of the Milky Way. There are smaller than him in the Army.'

Joe could have done without the hassle but he knew it was a problem that was going to crop up all through the tournament The birth cert would have to be produced. He decided to get on the phone to Eric's father and have Dave's dad bring the cert with him next day when he was coming to Sligo to bring the players home.

In the heel of the hunt, Tubbercurry lost by two points. They put in a protest on the grounds that Eric was overage, convinced that once the birth cert was produced they'd win the protest and proceed to the semi-final of the tournament.

Bull and a few others sniggered at the Tubbercurry protest and went off for a fed at Little Sid's Mobile Diner. Finished there, they watched some of the games.

Second game of the day for Shannon Harps was in the afternoon against Manor-hamilton. Bull, Dave and Rory were familiar with most of the team from playing them at schools' matches.

Joe played the same team as in the first match, only difference being that Eric the Viking was included from the off. At the start, he attracted a few hard looks from Manorhamilton but nothing more – they took Rory's word as to his age.

Rory was better known through playing for his school team in Leitrim than playing club football in north Roscommon for Shannon Harps. So Manorhamilton knew all about him and had great respect for him as a player. It was easy to see why. He dominated the game from midfield, pretty much in the same way as he had done for his school team all through the previous season. But not only that, it was obvious he was improving as a player with each passing month.

Quite a crowd had gathered for the afternoon sessions Although there was a match in play on the other pitch most of the crowd were attracted towards the Shannon Harps v Manorhamilton game. Initially the focus was on Eric the Viking, but in the end it all came down to Rory. His display was almost awesome, his catching and kicking ability a sight to behold.

Shannon Harps won by five points. But the real winner was Rory. Quite a lot of people took notice, not least an observer from the Roscommon Juvenile Board.

'Does he play as well as this all the time?' he asked Joe Duggan.

'Mostly. Sometimes he can be better.'

'He's fairly consistent then?'

'As consistent as rain falling in Kerry,' sighed Joe.

Before the throw-in on Sunday morning for the third game at group stage, Eric the Viking's birth cert arrived, courtesy 'express delivery' by Dave's father.

One problem solved!

Unfortunately, they lost the game by three points; they finished second in the group and had to face the winners of the other group (Ballina) in the semi-final.

That turned out to be a close-run affair. They lost by a single point: 1-5 to 1-6.

What was hard to take was that they had played really well — only to be robbed by a dubious penalty decision.

The same referee was in action again for the final between Ballina and the home team. He performed true to form and played a starring role for Ballina (*his* home team); they won the game by seven clear points

On the way home Bull said, 'I know Ballina won the tournament. But guess who the real winner was?'

'No. Who?' asked Rory.

'Little Sid and his nifty diner.'

'How come?'

'The ref robbed us and he robbed Sligo. But Little Sid robbed everybody with the prices he was charging.'

They all nodded in agreement.

Among all the amateurs, Little Sid had proved to be a true professional: the only one present at the tournament.

7 The Big Young Lad

While the U-13s of Shannon Harps had the excitement of the Sligo Feile Na Gael tournament, the U-10s hadn't the boost of any pre-season treat. They went straight into their league programme from the off. For James and Megan it was great to be playing at their own age level, especially for Megan because, at last, she'd have more than a good chance of getting a game every week. Jack decided to play her left-half-back, with James retaining his favourite position, top of the left.

Jack surprised most people in giving such a lot of his time to training the team and looking after them on match day. For years he had been more into pottering around his small hill farm than helping out with football clubs. But now that Shannon Harps was up and running he gave them his all, though he used Bull as his 'legs' to do most of the heavy work during training sessions.

Sometimes Helen Moran gave a hand,

especially on the days Big Mary and Stella were away on squad training with the county U-14 panel. The two girls had really made their mark during two trial sessions in Elphin and, as a result, they were now fully-fledged members of the county U-14 girls' panel. The whole process had come together very quickly for them.

Not so for Rory. He knew his name had been noted during the football tournament in Sligo, but he had heard nothing since.

The entire U-10 squad settled in quickly and they won their first four games. The first setback came in game five against a team from down the county that they had never heard of before

They would soon know all about them.

Even before the game there was an air that this was no ordinary club. The pitch was in the middle of nowhere, with not a house or a person to be seen for at least two miles. There were no dressing-rooms. And, very strangely, no nets, though the markers were in place. More importantly, there was, so far, no opposition. The only signs of life in that desolate place were the Shannon Harps players, the four cars they had come in, and a lone spectator.

'There's no sign of the other team. What are we going to do?' Jack asked him.

'Get togged out. There are still five minutes to the throw-in.'

'What if they don't show up?'

'They will. They always do. Worse luck.'

'What do you mean, worse luck?'

'You'll find out soon enough.'

Three minutes later the opposition cycled into the field on a varied assortment of bikes. They were already togged out except for football boots. Not that they came without them. They were laced together, hanging from their necks. First impression was of a tribe of wild children.

A big fourteen-year-old out in front was obviously the leader, if not the manager. Apart from his football boots he also had a length of heavy rope wrapped around his midriff. He made straight for Jack and introduced the referee who had come with the tribe.

'Just got here in the nick of time.' said the big young lad. 'Got the match card, ref?'

'Sure. Here.'

'What are you doing giving him the match card?' interjected Jack.

'Because he's the manager and he wants to fill it in.'

'Isn't he a bit young to be a manager?'

'Well, it kind of balances out. On the one hand, he's a bit young to be a manager. On the other, he's a bit old to be a player.'

'You mean he plays as well?'

'At centre-half-forward and everywhere else that matters.'

'He plays on this team?'

'Sure.'

'But this is U-10. He's overage.'

'That's not for me to decide. I'm only here to ref.'

The big young lad was busy filling in the referee's card with the names of his players, but that didn't stop him from making a speech: 'When I started playing football at first I wasn't very good. But I got better and better. I'd no boots, no togs. I had to get a loan off the team. In the end, I got so good the manager gave up and left me the lot. And now I run the show. How's that for progress?'

Jack and Bull couldn't believe their ears. Neither could any of the team. This was unreal. Cloud Cuckoo Land stuff.

'Ref, there are no nets,' complained Bull. 'Does that mean there's no game?'

'No, we'll play without them. No big deal.'

'Try this for size,' finished the big young lad handing Jack the referee's card. 'I'm off to get us ready for the match. We've played four matches so far and won all four. This will be our fifth win. See you on the pitch.'

Shannon Harps U-10s went into the game in a state of shock. The big fellow had lined out as bold as brass in the centre-half-forward position. Beside him, the Shannon Harps players looked like a row of skittles ready to be sent flying all over the field.

Megan was terrified she would come into contact with him. She wanted to opt out but Jack and Bull would have none of it. If they allowed her to leave the pitch, a few more would have wanted to follow. Shannon Harps would have ended up with half a team and a massacre to boot.

As it was the U-10s didn't do too badly, considering. But they were seven points down at the half-time break.

During the break Bull Malone grabbed the largest-sized jersey on view and told the ex-occupier he was going on in his place for the second half. It didn't matter to him that he had no nicks or boots. His rolled-up trousers and bovver boots would do the job just as well. It was time to sort out the big fellow. And Bull felt he was the man for the job.

'You can't go out there,' protested Jack. 'You'll only get us into trouble.'

'There'll be no trouble. The ref couldn't give a curse. Your man, the big fellow, is a plonker. Give me any sub's name on the ref's card, I'll use that. Come on.'

'Robert Fanning.'

Neither the big fellow, nor his team-mates, batted an eyelid when they saw Bull lining up for the second half. But when he scored two straight goals, breaking from about thirty

74

yards out and powering almost into the square, then it was time for the big fellow to bring a secret weapon into play.

Somehow the home team's crossbar broke. The referee halted play so as to decide what to do.

But the big fellow had the solution. He suggested that they extend the rope he brought to the match across the expanse where the crossbar had been.

The rope was quickly put in place with the ends hanging down to waist height, and the ref restarted the match.

The big fellow was in control of the umpires at the goal-posts. They were part of his U-10 squad and although they were non-playing members they were an important part of his game plan.

Shannon Harps were playing into the goal with the rope for a crossbar. Every time the ball was struck just below crossbar height the rope sagged and the ball went over the bar. Bull missed two further certain goals because of it. He now knew why there weren't any nets in place. If there had been, crossbar or not, the ball would have gone into the net and the two goals would have stood. The whole thing was a farce.

In rage, he shouted to the ref, 'What are you going to do about all this carry-on?'

'Not a lot. Just play the game out.'

'It's not on. You can't allow this messing to continue.'

'Maybe not. But there's nothing against it in the rule book.'

'My God!' bellowed Jack. 'I just can't believe it. Referee, what's your name?'

'It's not for me to tell. Anyway, it's on the match card. Protest if you like but with that big fellow *you* brought on at half-time it isn't worth your while. Just try and win the match, and leave it be.'

'And how are we supposed to do that?'

'Tell your team if they're shooting for goal to play the ball on the ground – just to be on the safe side.'

And that's what Shannon Harps did. It rapidly became a game of Bull v the big fellow, not to mention the rope.

Bull played a blinder and pulled Shannon

Harps from the jaws of defeat by winning the match by a solitary point.

James and Megan thought the big fellow would be a poor loser. Instead, he took it all in good stead, wrapped the rope around his waist, waved good-bye and cycled away at the head of his players.

Shannon Harps never saw them again. Two weeks later another team complained and they were thrown out of the league.

As for the referee, it was hard to understand how he had turned such a blind eye. But there was an explanation. Seemingly, he was the big fellow's father.

Not only was he the big fellow's father. The rest of the team were his nephews. Descended from the ranks of his innumerable brothers and sisters.

A few days later James and Megan called on Paddy Joe Padden.

He wasn't his usual self. He didn't have a whole lot to say. He was also moving a lot slower than usual.

'Are you sure you're okay?' asked James.

'Course I am. Nothing gets easier at my age. Though I wouldn't mind you bringing a few messages from the shop in the village every now and again. It would help if you dropped by every few days.'

'We could do that surely. Couldn't we, Megan?'

'Of course. We'll do any messages you want. We could even get the grown-ups to give a hand.'

'I wouldn't want that. The two of you are enough. I don't want a fuss.'

So saying, Paddy Joe told them to sit

down while he got a pot of tea ready. He had found it something of an ordeal, so Megan gave him a hand.

It was clear that there was something wrong with Paddy Joe. He just wasn't well.

Tea and biscuits over, he went to a press and took out the old rusty key he had shown them the last time. The one that had been brought back to the castle by the five long-departed brothers. He laid it on the table.

'I want you to have this key. It's a link with the past. So keep it safe. Safe as all the stories I've told you these last few years. Because I feel my time is running out.'

James didn't know what to say. 'There's divil a bit wrong with you.'

'If only that were so.' Paddy Joe smiled. 'What's the difference between May and July?'

James and Megan didn't understand the May and July bit. Someday, in the not too distant future, they would.

James took the key and put it into his pocket. It was almost too big to fit.

It would be looked after. They would both

see to that. They would keep it safe. Just as they would remember his stories.

As they were leaving, Paddy Joe asked them how their football team was getting on, then he went out to the road and watched them cycle off in the distance.

He thought of when he was a child and his father sent him out to the potato drill to dig potatoes with the one spade they owned.

The spade snapped and he stood in the drizzle, the tears streaming down his face, afraid to go back into the house and face the anger of his father.

After an hour his father came out and brought him home, broken spade and all.

He never said a word, just sat him at the fire and gave him a drink of warm water with sugar in it.

There was no such thing as football in those days.

Not for Paddy Joe Padden anyway.

8 A Cunning Plot

With every passing game, it was becoming clear that the U-14 team would be serious contenders in the league. Their only rivals were St Michael's and the townies. Already they had played St Michael's away from home and drawn with them. They hadn't come up against the townies yet, but it wouldn't be long. Another few weeks, and they would be away for the first leg.

Meanwhile, Rory and Bull had been called into the county U-14 squad. Their trainer was an army sergeant who travelled once a week from the barracks in Athlone to Roscommon town where the training sessions were held. He was a big red-haired man with a horse of a shout; nickname 'Red Hugh'. They played a few matches and did well against Sligo and Leitrim. But in their match with Galway, they took a walloping. Galway were different class. Totally.

At first, Rory found it hard to settle in with

the others. His shyness was a barrier. Dave saw what was happening and had a word with him. 'Don't let it get you down, Rory.'

'I just don't feel up to it…the talking bit.'

'Don't bother. Let your boots do the talking…on the pitch.'

'I feel as if I'm letting everyone down. They're expecting great things from me.'

'Relax. Just let it happen.'

Red Hugh was also keeping an eye on Rory. With patience and within four weeks he had talked him out of himself and settled into the team. Red Hugh could see Rory was star material – destined to play at the top level. There, shyness wouldn't matter.

Lately the townies U-14 manager had asked Stella and Big Mary for the low-down on Shannon Harps. But the girls were tight-lipped . They went to see Joe Duggan.

'So he wants you to spy on me!'

'No, he just asked us a few questions.'

'Like what?'

'Like how good the new players are. What kind of form is Rory in.'

'You'd think he'd come and do his own snooping. The cheek asking you two! You tell him nothing, only what I tell you to.'

'Like what?'

'Like Tommy Doran doesn't know much about football. That he's easily upset and is bound to get sent off.'

'But Tommy knows football inside out,' pointed out Stella. 'He keeps his cool all the time. He'd never get sent off.'

'That's so. But you tell that no-good townies' dope different. Tell him Tommy's a psycho. That his nickname is Man-o'-War.

That if he's laid into, he flares up and is a certainty to be sent off.'

'Anything else?' asked Big Mary, a big grin on her face. She could see what Joe was at. But Stella wasn't into it at all. She was beginning to feel uneasy.

'That Paudie is hardly worth marking, that's he's afraid and his nickname is Timid Timmons. Tell them we've a few other new players as well, but they're not a whole ton, nothing to be worried about. As for Rory, sing dumb. The townies know all about him anyway. Oh, and say Gerry Flynn really belongs to a team in the Westmeath League.'

'What team?'

Joe Duggan quoted a few lines of verse:

Last night I went to sleep in Kinnegad,
Free from Death and Danger,
Until Sergeant Reilly
Enlisted me to be a Connaught Ranger.

'We've never heard of a team called that. Where do they play out of?'

'They don't. There's no such team. The Connaught Rangers were a regiment in the

British army. They had a recruiting office about a mile from the townies' pitch. But those dimwits wouldn't know that. They know nothing. Just say Gerry Flynn plays for Connaught Rangers in the Westmeath League. There's sure to be a protest if we beat them. One other thing…'

'What?'

'Say Eric Higgins is overage.'

'But that's a lie.'

'So what? It's all lies. One more won't make much difference.'

Stella was shocked. (Martin would have been too if anyone had told him; but he never found out.) On their way home she said to Big Mary, 'We can't do what Joe wants.'

'Why not?'

'It's not fair.'

'So what?'

'The townies have been good to us. They've taken us in, got us on the county team. It's no way to thank them for all they've done for us. Let Joe Duggan do his own dirty work. I'm out.'

'Well, I'm not. Some of them still call me

names and it hurts. That's not fair.'

'The girls don't call you names.'

'The girls don't, but the boys do. I'm going along with Joe. I'll get my own back. I'll have the last laugh.'

'It won't be a laugh. It's sheer aggro. Don't do it.'

'I will. Are you going to play along?'

'No.'

'Then, I'll go ahead on my own. Only you say nothing. Keep out of it.'

'You bet I'll keep out of it. I want to know nothing about it.'

'Keep it that way. I'll do the damage on my own. A right horse-load of damage.'

Big Mary would do the damage all right.

The U-14 showdown against the townies duly arrived. It was an evening kick-off.

There was a lot of interest in the game. A convoy of five cars, plus Joe's Land Rover, left the village and took the narrow country road past the Lough Key Forest Park into town, on the edge of which was the pitch, the pride and joy of north county Roscommon.

None of the girls travelled. They must have got wind of Big Mary's plan to scupper the townies.

Dodgy McHale, the townies' manager, took a long hard look at the Shannon Harps players when they got to the pitch.

It gave Joe Duggan a right chuckle. Well, there was plenty to feel suspicious about in the case of Eric the Viking. Wasn't he a fine lump of a lad for thirteen years of age?

Dodgy was a big-shot forestry official who lived close to town. Originally from Crossmolina in Mayo, he thought he was God's answer to Paudie O'Shea, especially when it came to managing football teams. He had a few pre-match words with Joe.

'Fresh and well you're looking.'

'Thanks,' said Joe, wondering where this was all leading.

'Fresh and well your team is too.'

'They're a good bunch of lads for sure.'

'I hope they're not too fresh and over-cooked.'

'What's that supposed to mean?'

'Some of them look on the illegal side.'

'Illegal? Is that what you said?'

'Yes. Dodgy.'

'There's nothing dodgy about my team. All that's dodgy is yourself.'

'Is that so?'

'Yes, *Dodgy* McHale: That's your shoe size.'

'I'd be having none of that, you Roscommon sheep-stealer.'

'The cheek of you. And all those Roscommon kids on your team. Go on, you Mayo chancer.'

Things were really heating up between Joe and Dodgy. But Martin cut the chit-chat short. He got Joe out of harm's way and into the Shannon Harps dressing-room where he passed on the gist of his exchanges with Dodgy.

By the time they got out on the pitch the townies knew they were in for a rough time. Luckily, the referee had sized up the depth of ill-feeling and to prevent the game descending into a punch-up, he called them together before the throw-in and threw the rule-book at them. Any trouble would be nipped in the bud and he would abandon the game if he saw fit.

His words cooled matters and the game got off to a tough but rule-abiding start.

Right from the off Rory stamped his class on the game. The townies couldn't compete with his high fielding, accurate kicking and darting support play. He dominated the midfield to such an extent that the townies hardly got a look-in; they found it almost impossible to get their half-forward and full-forward lines into the game. And Bull terrorised their defence once he got anywhere near the fourteen-metre line.

Not that it was any better for the townies further out. Dave and Gerry Flynn sniped away from the half-forward line with crucial points which kept Shannon Harps marginally ahead, that's until Bull cut loose with two goals in rapid succession.

At centrefield, Paudie was quick to pounce on any broken play. He could have kicked long balls instead, but that would have been too easy. He really wanted to humiliate the townies and this he did by soloing through three or four players at a time before hand-passing the ball or shooting high for a few safe points. One felt he could just as easily have walked the ball into the net. Playing beside Rory in midfield had taught him a thing or two.

The townies never got off the mark at all. They were completely overwhelmed and outplayed. Beaten 5-13 to 1-4.

Eric Higgins didn't play in the first half; he came on during the second. Dodgy's eyes lit up when he saw him. Prior information or not, Eric the Viking looked a certainty to be overage. How could he be anything else, judging by the way the townies bounced off him every time they challenged for a ball? A definite protest there!

Dodgy had also taken note of Gerry Flynn, made sure his name was on the match card. One of the team had told him that he was suspect — wrong club!

All the Shannon Harps players were good on the day. They were a credit to themselves, Joe and Martin. There wasn't a bad player amongst them.

The strange thing about the townies was that they seemed to lie down after the first fifteen minutes, almost as if they had lost their appetite for the game and didn't really care who won.

After the match, Dodgy couldn't understand why his team had played so poorly; it was almost as if they weren't trying. But he got his explanation later when some of the players told him to slap in a protest against Gerry Flynn and Eric Higgins.

'That's just exactly what I'm going to do! What's the story on Gerry Flynn?'

'Plays for Connaught Rangers in the Westmeath League.'

'Who told you all this?' asked Dodgy.

'Big Mary,' was the answer. 'Sure we didn't need to win the match, so we didn't try. We'll win the protest and they'll get kicked out. So we were better off losing.'

'Did she say anything about not marking a fellow called Paudie?'

'Yeah, she said he was a heap of junk.'

Dodgy McHale's brow furrowed.

'What did she say about Tommy Doran?'

He was remembering an incident in the first half. One of the less aggressive of the townies had thumped Tommy – who didn't react. Instead the thumper was sent off.

'That he fights back if anyone lays into him. That he's sure to be sent off.'

Dodgy smelled a rat – a human rat!

Hats off to Big Mary. Although she now played for the townies, she was still Shannon Harps through and true.

All in all, it was a day to remember.

Even for Dodgy McHale. He felt bad

He would feel even worse when the protest was heard and the truth came out.

9 The Mystery Tour

The protest against Shannon Harps was heard two weeks later.

The townies lost hands down. It was a real double-whammy. They had taken Big Mary's low-down to heart and taken it easy, full certain the points would be theirs when it went to a protest. But now the two points were lost and their title hopes were dented as St Michael's had beaten them the previous week. Now it was a three-horse race between St Michael's, Shannon Harps and themselves.

Worst still, Big Mary's con job was the talk of the league. The townies' team felt everybody was sniggering at them while Dodgy McHale felt a right eejit. For weeks after he couldn't bear being around people. Luckily for him his job was mostly out in the open, in the forests and woodlands to be exact. So he was able to keep away from the critics and all those comedians who were having a laugh at his expense.

The fact that the protest had been made was a great tonic to Shannon Harps. It cleared the air. Now everybody knew that, colossal as he was, Eric the Viking was definitely underage. The speculation now centred on Paudie. Was *he* overage?

'He's from Arigna, you know.'

'So what?'

'That place is like the Wild West. Ever see the graveyard up there?'

'No.'

'It's on a hill. Just like Tombstone. I'd say that Paudie fella is a definite overage player. The strength and the power he has. It's unnatural for a thirteen-year-old.'

The league committee thought likewise. They asked to see his birth certificate. Satisfied, they handed it back and cleared him to play.

Soon as the dust settled over that protest there was one last humiliation for Dodgy McHale and the townies. Paudie was called into the U-14 county squad. A townie was dropped to make room for him!

Big Mary was expecting a backlash over

setting up the townies' U-14s. But the rest of the club, especially the girls' teams, got great mileage out of it.

'Mary's some character,' said one.

'See the way she sorted out Dodgy McHale and his team of big-heads.'

'No one could have done it better, that's for sure. The best laugh I've had in years.'

'You wouldn't want Dodgy McHale to hear you say that.'

'To hell with him.'

'He'd throw a wobbler.'

'Ever hear that song: "Big Mary keeps on rolling?"'

'No.'

'Well, it's about a river-boat on the Mississippi called Big Mary. Goes something like: "Big Mary keeps on rolling, Big wheel keeps on turning, Rolling, Rolling down the river." We could use the song as an anthem for Big Mary.'

'Forget it, she'd do her nut. Leave her be. At heart, she tries her best for our team.'

The townies weren't quite the club Big Mary, Stella and Shannon Harps thought they were. There was more to them than a U-14 team of big-heads. Big Mary's standing in the club proved it. She might be public enemy Number One with the U-14s. But she was a cult figure to the rest.

The two old-timers, Martin and Jack, got great enjoyment from the exploits of Shannon Harps.

The recent carry-on with the townies made them smile, although they didn't say so. Not publicly anyway.

They'd meet in a corner of *The Cross Bar* pub once a week and discuss all the latest football exploits and antics that were part and parcel of the Shannon Harps set-up.

Pranks from their own young days were suddenly remembered and spoken about.

'I remember when I was only ten,' said Jack, 'and oul' Packy Daly came to the village pump for a bucket of water. The bucket filled, he came in here and stood at the corner of the bar and had a pint of ale.

'Charlie Conlon came in not long after and got into the other lad's company. I was standing outside in the yard with a water pistol in me hand. I could hear every word going on. What's more I could see it all through the open window.

'I crept over to a corner of the window and every time Charlie turned away from Packy I sprayed his neck with water.

'Third time this happened, Charlie got into a rage. He was fully sure Packy was in some way squirting water from the bucket at him every time he turned his back.

'In next to no time they were at one another's throats. All hell broke loose.'

Joe had heard about a dream trip – at least he reckoned it to be a dream trip. Four coach-loads of old-timers were going on a trip to Lough Derg and as the fourth coach was only half-full, it would leave plenty of room for Shannon Harps U-14s at a knockdown price. It was due to leave Carrick-on-Shannon early on Friday morning, returning late Sunday night.

Joe put the idea of the trip to Dave but he wouldn't give the eventual destination, just in case Dave would be put off.

'Want to go on a trip?'

'Where?'

'It's a mystery tour. Mum's the word. Can't tell you until we get there.'

'How much is it?'

'Forty euro.'

'Forty euro is a bit steep for a day out.'

'It's not a day out. It's a whole weekend. Going Friday morning, back Sunday night.'

'That's not bad. Does it include bed and breakfast?'

'You could say that. It's going from Carrick. I have to know soon.'

'How soon?'

'The weekend. And I want the money up front.'

'Are the others going?'

'I haven't asked them yet. But I imagine all the team will want to go — I've put in for our weekend match to be postponed. Think about it and let me know tomorrow.'

The following day Dave and the rest of the team had their answer for Joe.

They were all going on the trip.

On Friday, everyone got to the meeting point in Carrick-on-Shannon at the time appointed. All four buses were already there. Apart from Shannon Harps, the mix was made up of farmers' wives, spinsters and old-age pensioners.

'Must be some drag of a place we're going to with this lot on board,' moaned Bull. 'Thank God it's a mystery tour. I hope we never get there.'

'I think it's a Legion of Mary outing,' whispered Dave.

'What makes you think that?' queried

Paudie from Arigna.

'There's a priest sitting up front on the first bus. He's not there for nothing.'

'Probably a trip to Knock,' groaned Bull.

'Or a hike up Croagh Patrick,' laughed Paudie. 'If I'd known I could have brought a tent and a billy-can. Anyway, what do you expect for forty euro. A weekend away is a steal at that price, even if it's Knock or Croagh Patrick. One sure thing, it's not Lourdes.'

'Why not?'

'We'd need a plane for that, not a bus.'

'You'll need to start hiding your crisps and cans of coke,' butted in Rory.

'Why? What do you mean?'

'Joe is taking them off all the lads getting on to the bus. Sweets, coke, crisps, sambos, the lot.'

'What's he doing that for?'

'How would I know? But he's doing it.'

'Hey, Joe?' asked Bull. 'What's with the confiscation?'

'You're supposed to be fasting from early this morning. No food is allowed. That's the rule.'

'Hear that, lads? We're on a fast! No wonder it only costs forty euro for the trip. Is this a pilgrimage, Joe? Are we going to be saying prayers all weekend?'

'You'll see when you get there. Just hand over anything eatable. I'll leave everything in the shop down the street. You can collect it when we get back.'

'This ain't for real, Joe! It can't be! Just tell me!'

But it was for real. They had to hand over the lot, except for the small items: a few Rolos, Smarties and stuff.

All of a sudden they wished they had told Joe they weren't interested in taking a trip. But they had paid forty hard-earned euro a head and the agreement was they wouldn't get it back. They all trundled on to the bus, miserable and downhearted, feeling they had been cheated out of not only the money but a fun weekend away from home.

'It's Croagh Patrick, Joe, isn't it?' wailed Bull.

'It's not Croagh Patrick, it's a mystery tour,' corrected Joe. 'Sit down and relax.

101

You'll know soon enough.'

'When?'

'When we get there!'

Ten minutes later the convoy of buses left Carrick and headed out of town.

Three miles out Dave made a statement: 'We're heading north. It's Lough Derg. It can't be anywhere else.'

'Are you sure?'

'Certain.'

'It's Lough Derg, isn't it, Joe?' wailed Bull once more. 'Isn't it, Joe?'

The reply was short and curt:

'Shut-up!'

Up the front of the bus a few pairs of rosary beads were being put to use.

There was no point in asking Joe any more. They knew the mystery destination.

It *was* Lough Derg.

Just short of two hours later the four buses arrived on the shore of Lough Derg. It was in the middle of nowhere. They had to go by boat over to the island, which was a mixed fortress of a church and a few other grim-looking buildings, with enough open space for pilgrims to walk around in their bare feet, in between fasting and going without sleep for the few days they would be on the island.

'They say if you last the distance you'll never go to Hell,' said Rory, by way of consoling them for the prospect ahead.

'We've already landed. This *is* Hell,' retorted Bull. 'Now that we're here our first priority is to escape.'

'Can you swim?'

'No.'

'Can any one swim?'

'Eric the Viking can.'

'Why doesn't he escape?'

'He doesn't want to. He likes it here. He's around the back doing press-ups and stomach exercises. Says it's a great place for self-motivation. Fasting appeals to him. Says it will strengthen his will-power. He's barmy. I know how we'll get off the island! We'll go down to the quay and bribe one of the boatmen to take us back to the shore.'

'It's a waste of time. Some of the lads have already tried. They said they'd only get into trouble with the monks.'

'Monks?'

'Yeah, there are a few monks here on a pilgrimage. They're keeping an eye out for us in case there's any messing.'

'I don't see any monks.'

'You're not supposed to. They're all too busy saying prayers.'

'Well, if they're too busy saying prayers the boatmen should have no problem taking us off the island.'

'That's where you're wrong. The boatmen are afraid of the monks. They say their eyes are everywhere. That if they take us off the island they'll only have bad luck for it. We'll just have to sit it out and do our time. There's no other solution.'

'I don't know how grown men can be afraid of monks. I'm not, never will be.'

But that was where Bull was wrong. The monks had had a word with Joe. They didn't like the idea of so many kids in the one group. They were afraid of the other pilgrims being disrupted from their meditations. They asked Joe to split the Shannon Harps party into three groups. The monks would take charge and supervise them for the duration. Joe agreed.

And that was the sum total of the forty-euro trip to Lough Derg: prayers, fasting, and more prayers, watched over by three monks who knew by heart every prayer and hymn that was ever written.

By the end of the three-day trip, everyone, Joe included, was either a saint or a wreck. Some even had a smattering of Latin.

Leaving Lough Derg Bull had only one thing to say: 'All good things come to an end. Thank God.'

Most of the lads nodded in agreement. Those who didn't were on the nod from a lack of sleep.

One certainty, Eric the Viking apart, no one would be going back.

10 Endings

Shannon Harps went on to finish the season in some style. Although the U-14s didn't win a trophy they went close. Joe was very pleased. It augured well for the following season; then the team would be all the stronger as they wouldn't have to give away a year in age Except for Paudie and Ned – they'd have to watch from the sideline.

All the players were pleasantly surprised when Martin's grandson Dara arrived from Athenry for a few weeks' holiday towards the middle of August. Dara got something of a surprise too when he saw how well they were playing and how much they had improved as footballers in the last year.

It wasn't long before they were asking how things were going for him on the hurling fields of Galway

Dara was modest about himself. Of course, he was playing like a house on fire. He was definitely one for the future, a certainty to hurl at county level in the not too distant future. And after meeting the Galway U-14 football team on the field both Bull and Rory were full certain that their U-14 hurlers were just as good.

If the season turned out well for the U-14s, it went even better for the U-10s. They won their league. That meant almost as much to Jack as it did to the players. He strutted about the village for weeks after, proud as a peacock. He even painted some of the fencing in the yard of his small hill farm in the Shannon Harps colours. The club presented him and Bull with a plaque apiece to commemorate the title win and as a thank-you for putting in such Trojan work preparing the team. Jack kept his next to an old framed photo Martin had found and given to him – one of Jack in the county squad before he departed the scene upset and bitter with the favouritism shown in the picking of the team.

James and Megan were thrilled with the team's success. But their joy was tinged by sadness, namely Paddy Joe Padden.

They had been out to visit him a few days previously and were alarmed by what they saw. He was barely able to walk, hardly able to look after himself.

Usually he brewed a pot of tea when they called. But this time, Megan did it for him.

But he could still remember the past.

'Four families of Paddens lived here all at one time. Three families gave up after the Famine. They had barely the price of their fares but they left for America. Nothing was heard of them again. The family that remained was my father's family. The small stone quarry at the back of the house is one of the quarries from where the stones were drawn to make the roads here. Some more slabs of stone were taken to Kilronan graveyard and left lying flat on the graves as markers. Some of them are there to this day, only covered over.

'There was a Harry Padden lived to be eighty. Died before I was born. They say he was soft in the head. Once summer came he sat day-dreaming under a bush above the quarry. The old people called the bush

"Harry Padden's bush". Harry is long forgotten, but the bush is still there. Things like that are worth knowing. Ah, when you're dying, what's the difference between May and July.'

James and Megan had heard Paddy Joe utter that phrase before. Only, now, they knew what it meant.

A week later they were out on the road.

Joe Duggan pulled up in his Land Rover.

'Have you heard?' he asked.

'Heard what?'

'Paddy Joe has been taken to the Plunkett Home in Boyle. They say he'll be better looked after there than living on his own.'

The news came as a shock to James and Megan. When they had seen him a few days ago, he hadn't said anything about going to an Old Folks Home.

When they got back to James's house they took out the old key Paddy Joe had given them.

They talked of the stories he had told them – and all the ones he hadn't.

They looked again at the key lying flat on the table.

James took it in his hand. But there was no lock to turn, nothing to open the past.

If not kept alive by James and Megan, Paddy Joe's old country customs and stories would fade quicker than daylight on a damp winter's evening.

Perhaps that was why Paddy Joe had given them the key.

Perhaps.

They went to the field, got Jimeen, and debated whether to go to the castle or down to the banks of the Shannon.

Then, in the full warmth of the summer sunshine, they headed for the Shannon.

Its water-filled blood would flow forever, legend, myth and reality intertwined as one.

In years to come the memory of Shannon Harps would become a blur.

But the Shannon would live on and on.

Forever.

SHANNON HARPS

This is the third *Shannon Harps*.

The first, *Shannon Harps 1*, is the story of how Joe Duggan got the team up and going.

The second, *Shannon Harps 2: Something New*, follows the fortunes of the team in their new community college – on and off the football field.

PETER REGAN was born in Keadue, County Roscommon, where, as he says, everyone either plays Gaelic football or is an enthusiastic follower.

His other books include the *Riverside* series and three books for older readers: *Urban Heroes*, *Teen Glory* and *Young Champions*